Peek-a

£5.99

Published by Grandreams Limited, 435/437 Edgware Road, Little Venice, London W2 1TH

Annual designed and illustrated by Jonathan Mitchell, John Timms, Tudor Reece, Matthew Boss and Tim Howe.

Contributing authors: Karen King, Pat Posner, Andrew Midgley, Jackie Andrews, Davey Moore ('A Nice Shady Place'), and Alex Hogg ('Jungle Tots' and 'What a Wintry Day!'). 'Tilly to the Rescue', 'The Long, Long Baguette', 'Coming Home' and 'Snowy Adventure' were adapted from original scripts by Andrew Davenport and Robin Stevens.

CARLTON

BOO!

This book belongs to ....

CONTENTS

SNOWY ADVENTURE

Here is a place that is
very, very quiet and
very, very white.
Where can it be?
Listen. What can you hear?
Look. What can you see?
Where can it be?
One...two...three...

"Peek-a-boo!"

It's the Tots and they're on an adventure!

"Oh là là!
Où sommes-nous?"
asked Tilly.
"I don't know where
we are," said Tiny,
"but it's very, very quiet
and very, very white!"
"La neige! La neige!"
"Yes, you're right, Tilly,"
said Tom. "That's all snow!"

"J'aime la neige," said Tilly, picking up a handful of snow.
"I love snow too," said Tiny.
"Look at all these funny
shapes our feet are
making in the snow."
"Ce sont nos traces
de pas," said Tilly.
"Our footprints!" said Tom.

"Look – my footprints,
your footprints, Tiny,
and Tilly's footprints."
"Brilliant!" said Tiny.
"Watch me make some more."
Tilly and Tom watched while Tiny stamped around in the
snow, making footprints.

"Look, I'm making footprints!" said Tiny. "This is brilliant! A real snowy adventure!"
"Yes! Let's all make footprints!" shouted Tom.
The three Tots marched through the snow making lines of footprints and singing a song:

Here we go, here we go
Altogether in the snow.
Altogether here we go
We're having an adventure!

Here we go, here we go
Making footprints in the snow
Altogether here we go
We're having an adventure!

"But if these footprints are the footprints that we are making," said Tiny, "whose footprints are those?" and he pointed into the distance.

Tom and Tilly looked to where he was pointing.
"I don't know," said Tom, "but let's follow them and see where they lead. This way!" All three Tots began to follow the other footprints into the trees.

"What can it be?" asked Tiny.

"Je ne sais pas," Tilly replied.

"I don't know either," said Tom, "but if we follow them we'll find out." So they kept walking.

Through the trees they found the answer to the mystery.

"Regarde! Une renne! Une renne!" said Tilly.

"You're right, Tilly," said Tom. "It is a reindeer."

The three Tots watched quietly as the reindeer ate its food.

Then Tilly said, "Ssshh! Écoute!"

The Tots listened very hard and heard the sound of lovely magical bells. "Oooh!" said Tiny. "Look!"

Something was just disappearing into the trees.

"Qu'est-ce que c'est?" whispered Tilly.
"That was...that was... brilliant!" said Tiny.
"Tots, I think that was you-know-who, I do!"
"Ooooh!" said Tilly and Tiny together.

"We really had a snowy adventure, didn't we?" said Tom.
"Oui!" said Tilly.
"The best snowy adventure I ever had!" said Tiny.
And they hugged each other.

SNOW ANIMAL

Can you guess
what snow animal
Tilly has drawn?
Join the dots to
find out.

11

MAKE A SNOWFLAKE

1 "I like snowflakes I do," said Tom. "I'm going to make lots of snowflakes and stick them on my window."
So he put a cup on a piece of paper, drew round it, and cut out the circle.

2 Then he folded the circle in half.

3 Then into thirds, so it looked like a triangle.

4 Tom cut little notches into the triangle and unfolded it.
"What pretty snowflakes," said Tiny.
"You are clever, Tom!"

Note to Parents: Remember to supervise children using paste and scissors.

12

Tilly

WHAT A WINTRY DAY!

One wintry day, Tilly, Tom and Tiny found themselves far from home.

"Oooh là là! Regardez!" squealed Tilly.

"Wow, look at that!" squeaked Tiny.

"That, Tots," said Tom, "is the sea."

Tilly, Tom and Tiny stood and looked out to sea. Grey sky and grey sea seemed to go on forever and ever.

"Wow, the sky is all grey and the sea is all grey, too!" said Tiny.

"Et regardez ici..." said Tilly, looking at her feet.

"What should we look at Tilly?" asked Tiny. He and Tom looked down as well.

"Oh, look!" said Tom. "Even the pebbles are grey!"

"Oh no," said Tiny. "Where has all the colour gone? I thought it was supposed to be all colourful by the sea."

"Yes," agreed Tom. "It's all sort of dull-looking."

Tilly gave a knowing look.
"Mais non," she said. "Il faut ouvrir les yeux et regarder."
"Open our eyes, Tilly?" asked Tom.
"But our eyes are wide open!"
"Non, vraiment ouvrir les yeux!"

"What, really open our eyes and have a proper look, Tilly?"
"Oui. Suivez moi."
Tom and Tiny followed Tilly along the beach.

Tilly stopped at some pretty little rock pools.
"Voilà!"

"What?" asked Tiny. "I can't see anything special, Tilly."
"Regardez!" Tilly insisted.

The three Tots knelt down for a closer look at the pool. Under the water was a different world.

First, Tom found a tiny, weeny, little blue sea shell which sparkled as he picked it up out of the water. "Tots, look at this beautiful sea shell. It's all blue and twinkly."

"Cor, brilliant. Look at this!" cried Tiny as he fished a long, dangly, bright green piece of seaweed out of the water. "It's green. My favourite colour! Ha ha!"

"Et voilà ma couleur preferèe," said Tilly, pointing out a little red crab. "Wow, a little crab which is your favourite colour, Tilly. Beautiful red!"

"Oh là là!"

"Cor!"

"Wow!"

called all three Tots as a shoal of brightly coloured fish darted across the pool.

"Vous voyez," said Tilly, "il ya beaucoup de couleur à la plage, si on sait regarder."
"Yes, you're right, Tilly. If you know how to look properly, there are hundreds of beautiful colours at the beach," said Tiny.
Just then the sun came out.

16

"Look, the sky's bright blue now!" smiled Tom.
"Yeah, and the sea's bright green!" giggled Tiny.
"Et regardez le soleil," said Tilly.
"Que tout est beau!"
"Yes, Tilly, everything is beautiful now."
"What a beautiful, colourful world."

Tom.

WHERE IS TOM'S CASTLE?

The Tots want to play in the castle, but they can't find it.
Can you draw the castle in the space below?
When you have finished, colour in the picture
with your crayons.

TILLY TO THE RESCUE

"Look! What's that funny place?" asked Tiny. He pointed to a big, grey stone building with towers and turrets and lots of high windows.

"That's a castle, that is," said Tom.

"Oh, un chateau," said Tilly.

"What's a castle?" asked Tiny.

"Er…a castle's got high walls and great big gates and smelly old dungeons for prisoners."

"Oh. Why does it have high walls and great big gates and smelly old dungeons?" Tiny wanted to know.

"Well, it stops people getting in, you see," said Tom. They all stared at the castle. It looked a good place for a game.

"I know," said Tiny. "Why don't we play a castle game?"

"Oh, oui!" said Tilly. "Un jeu de chateau!"

"That's a good idea, Tiny," said Tom. "But Tots, in this castle game, could I be king of the castle? I'd like that, I would."

"Yes, all right, Tom," said Tiny.

"And I'll be the prisoner in the smelly old dungeon."

"Et moi, je te sauvais, Tiny!" said Tilly.

"Oh yes, Tilly, you can come and rescue me!" laughed Tiny.

21

Soon Tom was strutting around the castle walls singing a king-of-the-castle song. Tiny sat alone in the smelly old dungeons. "Poo-ey! I don't like this horrible smell," said Tiny, wrinkling his nose. The dungeon smelt all musty-dusty. It was a little bit dark, too. "Help! Let me out!" he cried. But nobody came. So Tiny sang a little song to pass the time:

I'm a prisoner in the dungeons
But Tilly will rescue me soon.
If she doesn't come this morning
Then she'll come this afternoon!

As Tiny sang his song and Tom marched round the top of the walls, Tilly was coming towards the castle.

"Oh là là! C'est le chateau de Tom!" she called loudly. "Je vais sauver Tiny!" "You can't come and rescue Tiny!" shouted Tom from the battlements. "I'm the king of this castle and you can't come in!" Tilly laughed and ran to the big gates. But Tom had shut them! Tilly couldn't get in.

Down in the dungeon, Tiny was getting a bit fed up with being a prisoner and waiting to be rescued. "I think I'll go up and see if Tilly has come," he said.

He made his way up the huge castle steps, to the top of the castle, where he met Tom.

"Tiny! What are you doing here? You're supposed to be a prisoner in the dungeons."
"I don't want to be a prisoner anymore!" said Tiny. "It's boring. And where's Tilly? Why hasn't she rescued me?"
"She can't get in because I've shut the great big gates," said Tom, laughing.

Just then they heard Tilly shouting.
"What's she saying, Tom?"
"I think she said, let me in or it'll be smelly socks!"
"Smelly socks!" replied Tiny looking down. "Oh Tom, look! Tilly's got a catapult!"

23

Outside the castle, Tilly wheeled a great big catapult machine close to the castle walls.
Then she loaded the basket.
"Un...deux...trois...!"
A load of smelly red socks, smelly blue socks and smelly green socks came whizzing towards Tom and Tiny.

"Poo-ooh!" said Tom.
"Errrgh! These socks really are smelly!" giggled Tiny.
"This is disgusting!"
Tilly catapulted some more socks at them.
"Stop! Stop!" Tom shouted at last.
"No more smelly socks, Tilly. I'll let you in!"

Down the steps ran Tom and Tiny. Tom pulled open the big, heavy gates and Tilly ran in to meet them.
"Tiny, je t'ai sauvé, je t'ai sauvé!"
"Clever Tilly!" laughed Tiny, giving her a hug. "You rescued me with your smelly socks!"

"That was a really good game, Tots," said Tom. "But, you know, those socks were really very smelly!"
"It was a brilliant, smelly game!" said Tiny and they all laughed together.

MATCH THE SOCKS

Tilly's got all the socks muddled up now!
Can you help her sort them out?
Draw a line from each sock to its match.

MAKE TINY'S BINOCULARS

1 Look how Tiny made his binoculars to go exploring with. First he painted two empty toilet-roll tubes.

2 When they were dry, he stuck them together with paste.

3 Then he carefully cut out a hole on the outside of each tube, at the top. Finally, he threaded string through the holes and knotted it, so he could hang the binoculars around his neck

What do you think Tiny saw through them?

Note to Parents: Remember to supervise children using paste and scissors.

28

JUNGLE TOTS

"Peek-a-boo!" said all three Tots as they popped up their heads. "Où sommes nous?" asked Tilly. "Yeah, where are we?" said Tiny. "Ooh, it's all green and leafy," said Tom.

The Tots decided to go and explore. "Ooer," said Tom, "it's all a bit dark and spooky." "I'm a little bit frightened," said Tiny. "Oh là là!" said Tilly, "J'ai une idée." "You've got an idea Tilly?" "Oui." She called to the sac magique, "Sac magique, sac magique, aide nous s'il te plait."

29

Tiny felt the magic bag wibble and wobble and squiggle and shake.
As they watched, out popped special explorer clothes for the Tots. There were binoculars for Tiny, a telescope for Tilly and an extra big magnifying glass for Tom.

"Wow, brilliant!" said Tiny. "Now we are ready to explore. This place is so green and leafy it must be..."
"La jungle," said Tilly.
"Yes, the leafy jungle," said Tom.
"Off we gooooo!" cried Tiny.

The Tots made up a little song to help them with their exploring:

Tilly, Tom and Tiny
Great jungle adventurers
Tilly, Tom and Tiny
Who knows what we will find?

Suddenly, they heard an enormous ROARRR!

"Oh là là! Qu'est-ce que c'est?" asked Tilly.
"Ooer," replied Tiny, "what was that?"
"Oh, um...don't worry," said Tom, "I'm sure we just imagined it!"

"ROARRRR!" came the noise again.

"Vite, vite, vite!" squealed Tilly as she ran off to hide in a bush.
"Yes, quick, hide!" said Tiny.
"Wait for me!" cried Tom.

The three Tots hid in the bush very, very quietly, without moving.
"Something's coming!" whispered Tom.

They all stared as a giant cat walked slowly past them. "Ooh là là, un chat énorme!" squeaked Tilly.

"No Tilly, not a giant cat," said Tom, "that is a scary tiger, that is."
"He's beautiful!" said Tiny, softly.
"Oh, oui, magnifique!" said Tilly.
"I love tigers," said Tiny.

"Allez! Venez!"
"Yeah, let's go!"
"Let's explore the jungle some more."

The three Tots carried on their way. Tiny scouted ahead through his binoculars, Tilly peered hard through her telescope and Tom looked closely at the ground.

"Ah ha!" said Tom. "Look at these!"
"Oh là là! Des traces de pas!"
"Yeah, footprints. But look at the size of them, they are enormous! What sort of animal could make footprints like that?" asked Tiny.
The Tots were so busy looking through their binoculars, telescope and magnifying glass that they didn't notice they were about to walk into something BIG!

32

Tiny bumped straight into a big grey tree trunk, and then Tilly bumped into him and then Tom bumped straight into her! They all ended up on the floor in one giggly mess!

"Ha ha ha," said Tiny, "I didn't see that great big grey tree trunk!"

"Ho ho ho," said Tom, "that great big grey tree trunk is enormous, how could you miss it?"

"Hee hee hee," said Tilly, "mais attend, les troncs d'arbres ne sont pas gris!"

"Ho ho. What do you mean, tree trunks aren't grey? Of course they…" Suddenly the big grey tree trunk slowly moved.

"Argh!!! Tots, tree trunks aren't grey and they certainly don't move!"

The three Tots all looked up.

"Oh là là! Ce n'est pas un tronc d'abre, c'est un animal!"

"Yes, definitely not a tree trunk but an enormous animal!" said Tom.

"Yes, Tots," piped Tiny. "It's a gigantic, enormous, massive, huge...

...**Elephant**!!!"

The three Tots ran
away to hide.

"Phew,
that was a close one Tots!" said Tom.
"Je n'ai jamais vu un animal aussi grand."
"No, I've never seen an animal that big either, Tilly,"
replied Tiny.
"WOW, I love elephants," said Tom.
The three Tots sat down for a rest.

"Gosh, all this exploring is making me very hungry,"
said Tom.

"And we've eaten all the special explorer biscuits, too," replied Tiny.

Suddenly something yellow bounced off Tilly's head. "AIEEE!" squealed Tilly. Tom laughed and laughed...

...until suddenly something yellow bounced off his head. "OOWWW!" said Tom, "what was that?" Tiny laughed and laughed...

...until a whole pile of yellow things landed on top of him. Tilly and Tom laughed and laughed.

"OOOH!" said Tiny rubbing his head. "Hang on, I know what these are, these are bananas! It is raining bananas on our heads! Ho ho!"
"Mais d'où viennent-elles?"
"Yes, where did they come from?" asked Tom.
"Oh ho ho, look up there," said Tiny, pointing to the top of the trees.

"MONKEYS!" they all cried together. There at the top of the trees was a family of monkeys with long tails and shiny brown fur, and they seemed to be having a party, throwing bananas to each other.

"Just look at those cheeky monkeys!" said Tiny.

"Et regarde toutes nos bananes!"

"Yes, look at all our bananas," said Tiny, "just right for a banana jungle treat!"

"J'aime les singes!" said Tilly.

"I like tigers as much as you like monkeys, Tilly," said Tiny.

"And I love elephants," replied Tom.

"Yum yum yum," said the Tots as they munched away.

ANIMAL FUN

1 "I'm going to be a tiger. Grrr! grrr!" said Tiny. He took a paper plate and cut two holes for his eyes.

2 Then he painted it orange. He cut out two tiger ears, painted them and pasted them onto the plate. Next, he painted a black nose and mouth and some tiger stripes.

3 He took a piece of elastic big enough to go around his head and taped it to each side of the mask. Finally he put the mask on. "Grrr! grrr!" he growled, chasing Tilly and Tom round the garden.

Note to Parents: Remember to supervise children using paste and scissors.

LOST IN THE JUNGLE

Help! Tiny's lost in the jungle! Can you help Tilly and Tom work out which path they should take to find him?

Tiny

THE LONG, LONG BAGUETTE

"Peek-a-boo!"

The Tots found themselves in a funny kind of shop, with rows of shelves behind them and a long counter.

"Mmm!" said Tom. "What's that lovely smell?"
"Oooh. I don't know. It's nice, isn't it?" said Tiny.
"It's coming from these long things on the shelves."
"C'est du pain," said Tilly. "Ce sont des baguettes."
"It's bread," said Tom. "These are baguettes, they are."
Tiny laughed. "They're very, very, very, long, long, long, long bread, aren't they?"
"Yes, Tiny. Very long."
"Oui, très longues," Tilly agreed.

Just then the baker came into the shop. The Tots all hid behind the counter so he wouldn't see them. He filled the shelves with freshly baked baguettes, then turned and went back into his bakery. One by one the Tots looked over the counter.

"Where's he gone?" asked Tiny.
"Suivez-moi," said Tilly.
Tom and Tiny followed Tilly into the bakery behind the shop and hid themselves. From their hiding place they could see the baker at work.

41

The baker poured water and flour into the big mixing machine.

"L'eau et la farine," said Tilly.

"Cor, look at all that mixture!" said Tiny.

The baker poured something else into the machine.

"What's he putting in now?"

"That stuff's called yeast, that is," said Tom.

"Et du sel," said Tilly.

"Yes, and he's put in some salt, too."

The Tots quietly sang a little mixing song:

Mixing, mixing, mixing
Mixing it all through...

Suddenly, the machine stopped. The baker lifted out the dough and dropped it onto the table.

"He's made all that dough, he has!" whispered Tom.
"Yeah."
The baker quickly sliced pieces of dough and dropped them one by one into a roller machine. Long rolls of dough came out.

"Cor. Look at all those long, long wormy things!" Tiny giggled.
"C'est les baguettes," said Tilly. Tiny and Tom looked hard at the long rolls of dough. "They don't really look much like baguettes, Tilly," said Tom.
"No because...erm...they're all wormy and floppy," said Tiny.
They giggled.

The baker set aside the long rolls of dough and went out of the room.

"J'ai une idée!" said Tilly, excited.
"You've got an idea, Tilly?" asked Tiny.

Tilly crept up to the table and reached for three of the long rolls of dough. She put the rolls end to end and began to roll them.

"What are you doing, Tilly?" asked Tom.
"Yeah. What are you doing with the long wormy things?" chuckled Tiny.
"Je roule," she explained. "On les colle ensemble."
"Oh. You're rolling them, and sticking them all together," said Tom.
"Sticking them all together!" laughed Tiny.
Then he stopped to think a little bit. "Erm...why, Tilly?"
"Pour faire la baguette la plus longue du monde entier!" said Tilly.
"Oh, we're going to make the longest, long baguette in the whole wide world?" said Tiny. "Cor! Brilliant!"

Tom and Tiny helped Tilly to roll the longest, long baguette. As they rolled, they sang:

Rolling, rolling rolling...
...La longue, longue, longue baguette...

"There. All joined together," said Tom.
"Très bien!" said Tilly.
They looked at the long, long, long roll of dough which stretched right along the table.

Just then, the baker came back. He looked at the long piece of dough rolled out on his table. Where had it come from? But then he shrugged and put the dough carefully onto a very long tray and carried it over to the oven.

"Look, Tots," whispered Tom. "He's taken it over to that little cupboard."
"Il la met au four," said Tilly.

"That little cupboard is the oven, that is," said Tom. "He's going to bake our long, long, long baguette."
"Ooh."

When the loaves were ready the baker took a cloth and pulled out the tray of cooked baguettes from the oven. The wonderful smell of freshly baked bread filled the bakery again as he put the loaves on a tray to cool. Then he carefully took out the long, long, long baguette.

"Hey, Tots," gasped Tom. "Look!"
"Oh, regardez! C'est notre baguette la plus longue au monde."
"Yeah. Look at our longest baguette ever in the world!" laughed Tiny. "It's enormous!"

The baker picked up the new loaves, including the long, long, long baguette, and arranged them all on the shelves in his shop – except the very, very, very, long baguette which wouldn't fit.

There were some children waiting to buy some fresh bread. When they saw the long, long, long baguette they jumped up and down with excitement. That was the one they wanted! "Celui-la! Celui-la!" they shouted.

The Tots giggled. "They want our very long, long, long baguette, Tots!" laughed Tom.
"Yeah. We made that. The biggest baguette in the whole wide world!"

They watched the children leave the shop with their wonderful loaf.

"That is a long, long, long baguette!" said Tom.
"And it's going to take a long, long, long time to eat it!" said Tiny.

Our friend Donkey

A NICE SHADY PLACE

"Peek-a-boo!"

"Where are we?" asked Tiny.
"Écoutez!" said Tilly.
The Tots all listened very carefully.
They could hear the gentle sound of the sea.
"We're on a beach, Tots," said Tom.
"Il fait chaud!" said Tilly.
"Phew, yes! It's so hot I think I might have
to take off my lovely cardigan," said Tiny.

49

"Look, those children are wearing hats to keep them cool and that man's got a hanky like mine on his head," laughed Tom, "to keep off the sun."
"That donkey looks just like our friend Donkey," said Tiny. "Even he is wearing a hat to keep him cool."

"That family have got an umbrella," giggled Tiny. "But it's not raining!"

"That's called a parasol, that is," Tom explained. "It makes a nice shady place for them to lie in, so the sun doesn't burn them.
"What's that stuff they're putting on?" Tiny asked.
"That's special stuff people put on to stop the sun burning them. We ought to have some, otherwise we're all going to get frizzled!"
Tilly had an idea. "J'ai un idée!" she said.

"Sac magique!" whispered Tilly. "Sac magique!" The magic bag wriggled and jiggled a bit, then something wobbled out.

"A parasol!" said Tom. He opened it up, so they could all sit underneath it.

"And what's this?" giggled Tiny, holding up a fat tube. "C'est crème solaire, Tiny," said Tilly, and she unscrewed the tube for him to put some on.

"Cor! Sun cream!"
Tiny gave the tube a big squeeze and...

...splat!

The cream shot out all over his face. "Eurrgh!" and "Oops," said Tiny as the cream went all over Tom and Tilly as well.

"Tiny!" squealed Tilly.

"Look what you've done!" said Tom.

"Oops. Sorry, Tilly. Sorry, Tom. It won't stop coming out of the tube."
"Tiny. Put the top back on!" said Tom.

"Oh, Tiny!" laughed Tilly.
"Tu es banane, ha ha!"
"Well, at least now we won't get sunburnt!" Tiny giggled.

SAND PICTURES

1 Tilly has made a brilliant sand picture. First she drew a picture of Tiny on a big piece of paper.

2 Then she traced over it with a glue stick.

3 Next she sprinkled on some sand and shook off the loose bits.

"Voilà!"

Note to Parents: Remember to supervise children using glue.

WHAT A BUSY BEACH!

Can you see Tilly, Tom and Tiny?
Can you see some children
playing with a beach ball?
Can you find a rockpool?
Where is the family having
a picnic?

COMING HOME

"Peek-a-boo!"   It's Furryboo!

He has been sniffling and snuffling around looking for the Tots. Where can they be?

They've been away for such a long time that the house has become dusty and cobwebby. Furryboo has eaten almost all the biscuits!

Suddenly, Furryboo pricks up his ears. What can he hear?

We love our house
Our secret house
Home to our secret house

It was the Tots! Home from their travels.

We're coming home
We're coming home
We've been away
Now we're coming home
We love our house
Our secret house
Home to our secret house.

Tilly played her flute and Tiny laughed, as they all marched up and down.
"Come on, Tots!" called Tom.
"Home to our secret house!" sang Tiny.

"Donkey!" said Tilly as she saw Donkey.
"Donkey!" called Tiny, running towards him.
"Donkey!" said Tom.
They patted their friend and hugged him.
"Lovely Donkey, we have missed you."

"Ah. Come on!" Tom led the others to the house.
"Oh, de retour à la maison," said Tilly, looking round.
"Yeah. Home at last."

"Come on Tom, come on!" said Tiny impatiently as they waited for Tom to open the door.
"Oui, Tom!" said Tilly.
"Vite! Allez!"
Tom took out the big key and unlocked the door.
They all looked inside.

"Look at our house!" whispered Tiny.
"Oh, regardez! Les toiles d'araignèes!"
"Oh, yes. Look at those great big cobwebs!" said Tom.
"Cobwebs everywhere," said Tiny.

Tom took a deep breath and blew the dust off the table.
They all spluttered and sneezed.
"There's dust everywhere, too!"

"Here, look at all these little footprints," said Tiny, pointing to the table.
"Oh yes. Something has been walking all over our table!" said Tom.
"Mais, qui à marche sur notre table?" asked Tilly.
"And look! Who's been tangling up all our telephones? They're all tangled together," said Tiny, holding up all the knotted wires.

"And Tots!" said Tom.
"Yeah?"
"Who's been eating all our biscuits?" He held out the empty biscuit tin for them to see.
"Oh!"
"Oh là là!"

"Do you know what?" said Tom after a moment, "I think we've been away so long our house has gone to sleep."

"Oh yes," said Tiny. "We should wake our house up, shouldn't we?"

"Yes, I think we should."

"Attendez, regardez!" said Tilly, and she began to play her magic flute.

As they watched, the curtains and windows opened by themselves. The dust all disappeared. The telephones untangled their wires...and in the garden, beautiful flowers appeared.

"Et voilà! C'est magique!" laughed Tilly.

"Cor, Tilly. That really was magic!" said Tiny. "Our magic, secret house is all awake now."

"Tots, we really are home now!" said Tom.

"Yeah!"

"Oui, Tom!"

We're home, we're home
We've been far away
We've seen lots of things
But we're home now to stay
We love our house
Our secret house
We're home, home, home!

WHERE SHALL WE GO? WHAT SHALL WE SEE?

Join the Tots as they journey to faraway places. You will need dice and a coloured counter for each player. Take it in turns to throw the dice and move around the board. The first one to reach home wins the game.

Have fun!

START

1 A beach! The Tots make sand castles. Miss a turn.

2 Cor it's hot! Miss a turn and put on a sun hat.

14 Where's Tiny? Go back three squares to look for him.

15

16 A la neige! Have a snowball fight and miss a turn.

17 Sledge forward two spaces.

18

19 Brrr! Pretend it's cold and chatter your teeth.

20